As the Earth's winter gets colder and colder, Professor Gamma realises that a powerful villain must be at work. He sets off for a distant planet to find the culprit, knowing that it will be a very dangerous task...

To Samantha

Titles in Series 823

First edition

© LADYBIRD BOOKS LTD MCMLXXXII

THE FROZEN PLANET OF AZURON

by Fred and Geoffrey Hoyle
illustrated by Martin Aitchison

Ladybird Books Loughborough

The Frozen Planet of Azuron

As the snow fell steadily against the window, William tried to study the flakes through an old scratched magnifying glass he had found in the tool shed. He wanted to be able to see the tiny individual crystals that make up a snowflake, but he wasn't having much success. "Some Christmas holiday!" he thought crossly as he looked out over the thick blanket of white that lay over the countryside.

Suddenly he decided he just couldn't stand being cooped up in the house any longer. Beside which, he'd had a good idea. He would go outside and search for wolves. In the last few days there had been reports on television about wolves escaping from captivity.

Although these stories had been denied by the government, William thought he would try to discover the truth of the matter for himself.

He had been looking at a book called *Animals of the World*, which showed the kind of footprints left in the snow by wolves. He knew that to be an expert tracker he had to study his quarry carefully, because he'd read that too.

The snow was still falling hard as he pulled on a pair of overtrousers.

"Where are you going?" asked his mother.

"Out!" said William.

"What, in this? You'll catch your death of cold!" his mother remarked, although she knew that once William had made up his mind it was difficult to dissuade him.

"If I have any bother, you can always follow my tracks in the snow," William replied cheerfully.

He drew the cords of his anorak tight as he stepped outside into the blizzard. Snow whirled in flurries around his head, making it difficult to see where he was going. The wind had drifted the snow into deep banks, and William found himself sinking up to his waist as he struggled even to reach the bottom of the garden behind the house. He remembered however that real trackers, like himself, simply revelled in these conditions, and he kept going. A true tracker always got his animal, no matter what the state of the weather!

As he dragged himself across the field that led from the bottom of the garden to a wood, William tried to think of a plan of action. Nothing special occurred to him, except that he must keep a wary eye out for his particular enemy, Foxy the gamekeeper, who was just the sort of person to be out prowling the countryside, even in a blizzard like this.

The tall trees of the wood gave some shelter from the driving snow, making it less difficult to search for wolf footprints. All William could find for a while were bird tracks, but then at last he came on the paw marks of an animal of some kind.

Each mark had four neat round holes, and since the holes had not been filled in yet by the falling snow, William knew they must be very fresh. He examined one of the marks carefully with his old magnifying glass, but this didn't really help him to identify the animal that had made them.

The tracks led deeper into the wood, to where a narrow path between the trees led upwards towards the open Down which lay above William's home village. The paw marks stopped half way along this path, and there, near the base of a tree, lay the body of a red fox.

There was nothing to suggest how the unfortunate animal had died. William reached down to pick up the fox by its tail, and as he touched it, there was a burning sensation in his hand. With a cry of pain he dropped the corpse, and as it hit the ground the remains of the fox shattered into a million pieces!

A strange sound rising above the wind made William forget the pain in his hand. The sound grew until he was able to recognise it as the panting of some large creature. A shiver rippled down William's spine as he searched for a quick route of escape from the thick wood. An idea flashed into his mind. As the panting grew louder and louder, he took off as quickly as he could in the direction of Wit's End, the house where his friend Professor Gamma lived.

William pushed his way through the deep snow, so fast that his heart began to thump in his ears. Loud as this was, he could still hear the heavy breathing of the creature behind him.

The nearer he came to Professor Gamma's house, the stronger grew the wind, slowing him down more and more. With a last desperate effort, William jumped over the garden gate, and only then did he turn, just for an instant, to look behind him.

Bounding towards the gate was the most enormous dog he'd ever seen! It was a shining brilliant white, except for its bright red tongue, lolling to one side of its mouth. The dog, flashing almost like a piece of crystal, was at least the height of a man. Red drops of saliva dripped from its jowls — and as they hit the ground, the droplets exploded with a sharp cracking sound.

"William!" cried an anxious voice. He turned to find
Kiryl, the Professor's young daughter, running towards
him. She was carrying a garden spade, and she shouted
wildly, "Run for it!" Then she hit the huge animal

time after time with the sharp edge of the spade. Suddenly, the spade itself fragmented into a cloud of mist. The dog was blinded for a moment, and in the confusion, Kiryl grabbed hold of William and pulled him into the kitchen of the house at Wit's End.

It seemed safe in the kitchen. Two enormous chairs flanked the large old-fashioned fireplace, where flames leapt around burning logs in the grate. There was a heavy scent of wood smoke in the air.

"What *was* that?" William asked.

"I don't know," replied Kiryl. "I only wish Father was here."

The kitchen door rattled violently. It was a big heavy wooden door, yet it bulged visibly in its frame as the enormous dog pushed against its outer side.

"When will your father be back?" William asked again, anxious in his turn, as he moved closer to the fire.

"I'm not sure," replied Kiryl in a small nervous voice. "He just said he was going to find out why we're having so much snow."

The door rattled violently again, and a biting fierce wind whipped through cracks in its wooden frame. Then the shrill whistle of the wind changed suddenly into a cackle of distant laughter. At this, William picked up a long iron poker from the fireside.

"I'm ready for them now," he said, more bravely than he felt, and he stood by Kiryl's side in the middle of the kitchen.

Behind them the roaring fire gave a momentary surge — then went out, just as if someone had turned it off with a switch. At the same moment, the door blew violently open. In came the great dog, its eyes blazing brilliantly like two enormous diamonds. Snow blew into the kitchen in a thick white cloud, settling on everything, including the snuffed-out logs in the fireplace.

Trying to be brave, William moved forward and struck the brilliant white dog hard with the poker. But the animal — if it was an animal — seemed like a piece of tough rubber, for the poker simply bounced off it. All William had for his effort was a burning pain in both hands, as if they had been burned by the poker handle.

Kiryl screamed in terror as the great dog pounced upon her. William tried to throw himself at the dog, but he was hit violently by an unseen force, which threw him to the far side of the kitchen. Then, as he climbed slowly to his feet, a still more astonishing thing happened. The dog faded from its flashing white into a dull grey, and everywhere over the kitchen there was a deathly silence, with Kiryl standing rigid in the middle, a completely frozen figure.

Into the room slipped a vague shadow flowing restlessly this way and that, until at last a shape took form. William had never seen a ghost, but if he had he was sure it would have looked just like this. It was a humanoid, dressed in a large flowing cape and carrying a carpet bag. This unearthly figure stopped at Kiryl's side and opened the bag. William was unable to move as he watched the ghostly creature proceed to stuff Kiryl's body into the bag. As if this wasn't enough, the shadowy form also flowed into the bag, until it too was all gone. Then, in a sudden glow of light, both the carpet bag and the now lack-lustre dog vanished without trace.

William went on standing still for several minutes, until a flurry of snow blowing through the open door brought him back to his senses. He moved slowly to close the door, aware again of the pain in his hands. Outside, the blizzard was raging even more wildly than before. A dark figure appeared through the snow as William was about to close and bolt the door, and he recognised the big shaggy form of Kiryl's father, Professor Gamma.

"You look as though you'd seen a ghost, young man," Gamma said as he reached the doorway.

William stared at the Professor, a big lump forming in his throat. "That's just what I *have* seen. A ghost. It's taken Kiryl away," he blurted out.

Gamma closed the outer door firmly, then put his arm around William's shoulder, drawing him back into the kitchen.

"I thought some monkey business was going on," the Professor said quietly, as if to himself.

William looked up and was surprised to see that, instead of its usual purple colour, Gamma's face was covered with what looked like soot. The more William looked at the Professor's face and clothing, the more he became convinced that Gamma had been rolling in coal dust.

Gamma sat William down in one of the tremendous chairs that flanked the fireplace, then he sat down himself in the other chair and listened as William poured out the story of the ghostly shadows and of the huge white dog. As William talked, he couldn't help noticing a curious metal box on the arm of the Professor's chair. It seemed to be jumping around of its own accord.

"I thought as much," remarked Gamma when William had finished. "There was definitely too much snow about."

"What does it all mean?" asked William, blowing on his hands as he still tried vainly to relieve the burning in them.

"How forgetful I've become!" exclaimed Gamma, jumping from his chair and leaping almost all in one movement to a kitchen cupboard, from which he took out a bright green bottle.

"Stopfrost," he explained, holding the bottle up so that William could get a good look at it. "Better give you a big dose. It's cold that's been causing all this mischief."

William eyed the emerald liquid that Gamma was pouring from the bottle into a spoon as long as a soup ladle. "What does it taste like?" he asked.

"Try it and see," the Professor told him.

William took a small sip to begin with.

The thick bright green stuff had a frightful taste, but no sooner did William manage to get some of it inside him than the pain in his hands disappeared. So, holding his nose tightly, he forced himself to swallow the rest of it.

"You see, it does help!" laughed Gamma. "Stopfrost was invented by a fellow called Zero, who I reckon is at the bottom of all this hanky-panky."

"Who's Zero?" William naturally wanted to know.

"Absolute Zero," explained Gamma. "Known as Abe Zero to his friends, of whom there are fortunately very few. The world could have managed very well without his genius."

"Why is that?" William asked again.

"The fellow discovered how to convert heat into action. All kinds of action, and he did it with perfect efficiency. It would have been fine if he'd kept the thing to his own laboratory, but he insisted on spreading it all over the universe, putting a lot of people out of their jobs."

Gamma was back now in his enormous chair. The metal box was once again hopping about on the arm of

the chair. Although he couldn't take his eyes off the strange box, William still managed to listen to what the Professor was saying.

"That was only just the beginning of the troubles caused by Zero," Gamma went on. "Perhaps his worst invention was a terrible affliction called entropy. Wherever you looked, entropy was always increasing. It just went on and on growing, choking everybody. Only Zero himself was immune from it."

"So what did you do?" William managed to ask.

"Several of us got together and decided enough was enough. With a trick or two, and a bit of thinking, we managed to banish Zero to Black-hole Space."

"Black-hole Space, where's that?" William's voice had become loud in wonderment.

"Inside that carpet bag he carried. Where else could it be?" Gamma replied.

"But how could there be anything much inside that bag?" William wanted to know.

"Ah!" responded Gamma, shifting in his chair so that his spine cracked loudly. "The bag is like a door. Open it, and you fall into a new world. Remember that a black hole may look tiny to someone on the outside, but to someone inside it can be enormous."

William nodded, as if he understood what the Professor was saying.

"What happened to Kiryl?" he asked, trying to give a more practical twist to the conversation.

Gamma was not to be deflected, however. "Zero managed to escape from Black-hole Space," he continued. "By his cleverest trick to date. By creating a system of virtual pairs. Something none of us had ever thought of, I'm afraid."

"But what happened to Kiryl?" William persisted in a firm voice.

"Don't be so impatient, young man," the Professor answered calmly. "I'm coming to that in a moment. You see, being imprisoned in Black-hole Space gave Zero a lot of time to think, which has made him even more dangerous than before. He's trying now to get all his old enemies into that carpet bag..."

"So he captured Kiryl as a sort of decoy?" William broke in excitedly.

"Exactly," nodded Gamma. "He knows I'll be after him, and he'll be waiting out there, doubtless with some new trick. Perhaps something to do with the energy pathways."

William knew about the energy pathways that went criss-cross all over the Universe, because he'd been on them himself. The ride could be a lot of fun, provided you were careful not to materialise with your head on one side of the galaxy and your body on the other side.

"What can Zero do about the energy pathways?" he wondered.

"Mess them up," the Professor answered promptly. "Zero is sucking up heat in enormous quantities wherever he goes. He'll be using the energy he gets from it for no good purpose. You can count on *that*, my lad."

With these explanations concluded, Gamma lapsed into silence. It was the strange silence which always preceded their being launched from the Earth into the universal pathways. William watched as the Professor produced a huge pipe from a pocket of his jacket, the energy pipe that was really a communications switch.

The Professor also produced a box of matches and lit the pipe in the usual way. While he was puffing as hard as he could, with the pipe making a bit of a crackling sound, the lid on the metal box, which was still on the arm of Gamma's chair, popped open. A minute black sphere jumped out. The sphere immediately started to grow bigger, and in no time at all it was the size of a golf ball. In half a minute it was the size of a football, at which stage it exploded gently, showering clouds of small black particles all over the kitchen − all of which started to grow too.

"Botheration take it!" cried Gamma.

"What are they?" asked William as he ducked away from hundreds of rapidly growing black spheres.

"Better get out of here," grunted the Professor, "before we're drowned in carbon molecules."

"Where did you get them from?" William asked again, as they hurried quickly out of the kitchen into the hall.

"You'll find them all over the universe. They grow everywhere," answered Gamma.

There was a loud bang, and a giant molecule which had escaped from the kitchen burst apart, covering them with soot. In the next instant, everything vanished in an energy flash which lifted them from Earth on to the energy pathways.

"Where are we going?" asked William as they sped, house and all, through deep space.

By way of an answer, Professor Gamma, pointing through the hall window, said, "See that long cloud over there, just below the bright star Sirius?"

William nodded. "You mean the dark belt that's blocking out the stars behind it," he said.

"That's it. Well, unless I'm very much mistaken, that's a condensation trail of ice particles left by our friend Zero. Wrap that stuff around a planet and you'd block out all warming light and heat. Next thing you'd know, the planet would freeze up solid."

"Like an ice-age?" William suggested.

"Precisely so," replied Gamma. "That's just another of Zero's little tricks — causing ice-ages on planets he dislikes."

"Is that what was going on on the Earth, with all the snow and wind?"

"Can't be the slightest doubt about it," Gamma grunted in reply, emphasising his opinion with a sharp crack of the spine.

They journeyed easily along the energy pathway, unlike some of the violent switchback rides William had had before. Occasionally they encountered brilliant cascades of sparks, where magnetic waves from side channels intermingled with the main force field, but these were not dangerous and did not hinder their journey.

"That's where we're going," cried Gamma eventually.

Ahead of them a sparkling white planet lay to one side of a star. As they drew nearer, more planets, less brilliant than the first one, could be seen orbiting the star.

"Where are we?" asked William.

"The star is called Hasmon, and the bright planet is called Azuron. You can look them up in the catalogue. It's sitting on the table beside the telephone in the kitchen," came the Professor's reply.

In the next instant they had materialised on the surface of the planet Azuron. William now understood why they had needed the Stopfrost, for it was so cold that otherwise they would soon have been frozen solid. They were still in the hall of the house, which had also materialised. They could hear a thumping noise from the kitchen — the carbon molecules were still growing, and they knew it would be a good idea to avoid them.

Gamma led the way from the hall to the french windows in the sitting room, which on Earth had overlooked a small snow-covered lawn but which now gave a splendid view over the brilliant white snowfields of Azuron.

"Is this what an ice-age on Earth would look like?" William asked.

"Yes, indeed, except that ice-ages on Earth have not been quite as total as this," replied Gamma, playing with his pipe and also attempting to keep the lid on the metal box from which the carbon molecules had

escaped. "When an ice-age is as complete as this, there is no way the light and heat fom the star Hasmon can get at the planet. The light is being reflected like a giant mirror. So everything stays completely hard-frozen. Another of Zero's tricks, I'm afraid," added the Professor as he managed to wedge the metal box under his arm.

"This is where Zero is living?" William asked again.

"Yes!" came the crisp reply. "On the dark side of the planet we'll find that carpet bag, with Zero lurking somewhere inside it."

"What happens when that side of the planet turns towards Hasmon?" William persisted.

"The bag opens. It sucks in light and heat to supply the energy which Zero needs to escape from the bag," answered Gamma without hesitation. "Boring life, really," he added as an afterthought.

"I still can't see how we can get Kiryl back," said William gloomily.

"You are a young man of little faith!" the Professor replied.

Almost as if someone had been listening to their conversation, a breeze whistled through cracks in the frame of the french windows, just as it had done before around the kitchen door. The breeze increased quickly to a hurricane wind, a wind that moved the house bodily over the icy surface of Azuron at an ever-increasing speed. Irregularities in the ice caused the house to spin like a top, making the ride distinctly unpleasant for its two inhabitants.

"Very funny! Very funny!" grunted Gamma, as his large body was thrown about the room for the hundredth time.

William felt quite sea-sick. He tried closing his eyes to cure the giddy feeling, but then the crashing of glass and timber caused him to open them again. There in the room was the great dog, not faded as William had last seen it, but brilliantly white and sparkling as it had been in the beginning. The dog bit furiously at the Professor, who to William's horror became still and rigid, just as Kiryl had done. Then it was William's

turn. The dog leapt at him, the same strange red liquid
dripping from its huge teeth. As they hit the floor, the
droplets exploded like small bombs, just as they had
before. Just as the dog's jaw closed about his shoulder,
William realised that the wind had dropped, and that
the house was stationary again.

Nothing happened — nothing at all. Only then did
William realise that the intention wasn't to chew him
up but to freeze him by an injection from the dog's
teeth, which were really enormous hyperdermic
needles. This hadn't happened, however, because of
the Stopfrost. He was just about to say so when he
caught a warning glance from Gamma. So William did
his best to make himself as stiff as a statue, the way that
Gamma had done. In that very moment, there came
the same cackle of distant laughter that he had heard
before.

It was not long before a ghostly figure approached
the french windows, a figure carrying a carpet bag.
There was no sound as it opened the french windows
and slid inside the house. William waited, his heart
beating loudly in his ears as the strange form in a large
flowing cape circled about them. At last it stopped in
front of Gamma and opened the carpet bag. William
was wondering if Gamma would allow himself to be
stuffed into the bag when the Professor suddenly
grabbed the ghostly arm that reached towards him.
The moment there was contact, every scrap of colour
drained from Gamma's body. He too became a ghostly
figure, part of another world, a world of shadows.

William watched in amazement as the two ghosts fought for control of the carpet bag. As they wrestled with each other, they kept changing their sizes and shapes. And Zero used his flowing cape like a matador in a bull-fight. Whenever he waved the cape, there was a clanging noise like the distant sound of a deep-toned bell, but otherwise the fight was quite silent. It took them through the french windows on to the snowfield outside.

The carpet bag was always at the centre of the fight, with each ghost trying to stuff the other one into it.

As he was about to follow them, William spotted the Professor's great energy pipe lying on the house floor beside the metal box from which the carbon molecules had emerged. Without hesitation, William picked up both of them, although he couldn't quite see what he was going to do with them. Then he went out through the french windows.

No sooner was William on the bright snowfield than the wind sprang up again, catching the pipe which William was holding loosely and sending it crashing to the hard snow. It was surprising how much noise the pipe made in its fall. William sprang forward and placed his foot firmly on it, so that it would not skid away in the wind.

Just then, when William was off-balance and off-guard, the flashing white dog re-appeared. It made a huge pounce — not on William himself but on his foot as it held down the pipe.

By good luck, the wind came to William's aid. A fierce blast blew both him and the dog helter-skelter along the icy snowfield. In the scuffle William managed to lift the pipe with his hand, and to push the stem of it into his mouth. Instantly, a cloud of black particles burst forth from the metal box, which William had pushed without thought into a pocket of his jacket. The particles settled like a pall on to the dog, which rushed frantically hither and thither, trying to shake off the sticky carbon. But the particles grew so quickly both in size and number that, no matter how many of them the dog managed to shake off, the animal was soon entirely covered from head to paws.

To William's astonishment, the great dog now started to steam like a village pond on a cold autumn morning. Water ran from its back, dropping with an audible plopping sound on to the ice. The black carbon was absorbing the light and heat from the star Hasmon, and the dog, since it was a zero-temperature dog, simply melted away, leaving behind nothing but a dark pool of liquid.

The long drawn-out wrestling match between the two ghosts was still going on, but it was beginning to look as though the Professor might be losing the contest, for his shadow was three-quarters of the way inside the carpet bag.

What with Gamma apparently losing the battle, and the constant uproar ahead as the carbon molecules from the metal box continued to multiply themselves, William became confused, and didn't know what to do next. He could see the situation was distinctly bad, for Zero's arm was now stuffing the Professor's head into the bag.

William puffed hard on the pipe, but that didn't seem to produce any help for Gamma. So in his nervous state William stuck his hands deeply into his trouser pockets, finding there the old scratched magnifying glass with which he had thought to track a wolf (which now seemed a pretty tame thing to have tried to do).

The melting away of the huge white dog suggested to William the idea of focusing Hasmon's light on to the ghostly shadow of Absolute Zero. Nothing happened for a brief moment when he first tried it, but then came a sudden puff of smoke, and a sickly sweet smell.

Zero must have been stung by the hot searing heat from the star, for he dropped the carpet bag to swing round sharply on William, who hadn't time to dodge a mighty blow on the head. The strong arm of Zero swung once more, but this time William managed to duck smartly and the arm rushed like the wind above him.

William had ducked so low that he was able to see into the carpet bag, and could see the shadows of Gamma and Kiryl emerging from it. Now Zero grabbed William by the arm, in just the way Foxy the gamekeeper did sometimes. Thinking of Foxy, he lashed out with a foot, and he found himself free once again.

The Professor and Kiryl were almost out of the bag now, and were both beckoning him urgently. Just as in a game of rugby, William ran around Zero and seized hold of Gamma's outstretched arm. The instant he took hold of it, the Professor's hand became visible again in its true colour. Whether this had anything to do with the pipe William didn't know, but he kept the

pipe still clenched between his teeth as he helped to pull his two friends from the ghostly world of Black-hole Space.

As he saw what was happening, Zero dived into the bag and began to pull Kiryl in the opposite direction, towards Black-hole Space. William now felt a great resistance to his effort. He closed his eyes and imagined himself to be a vast tractor pulling a heavy load. The more he made himself believe he was a tractor, the better progress he made. Suddenly, with two loud plops, like corks drawn from bottles, Gamma and Kiryl were out into the real world, standing there beside him.

"Well done!" the Professor gasped, breathing hard. "Getting us through that event was no easy job."

When he had recovered his breath, Gamma shouted, "To the kitchen, quickly!" He ran swiftly to the house, his spine creaking at each long stride, and it took him but a moment to throw the kitchen window wide open. Out billowed one dense black cloud after another. They were the carbon molecules which had been multiplying all the time. The black carbon settled everywhere, over the ice-covered ground of the planet Azuron, and over the carpet bag.

An agonised shout came from the carpet bag, as heat from the star Hasmon started to warm it.

"Let that be a lesson!" roared Gamma in reply to the shout.

Then a voice called out faintly, as if Zero were a long way off, "I'll get you all for this one day! I'll be revenged on the whole pack of you." Without warning, the carpet bag vanished in a faint dull glow of red light.

"He's really gone this time. There was a big red shift on that bag," remarked Gamma.

"Back to Black-hole Space," suggested William.

"Thank goodness!" said Kiryl. "It was terrible to be in such a huge empty blackness."

"Is that really what it was like in the bag?" William asked.

"Yes, a huge empty blackness," Kiryl nodded emphatically.

William still couldn't quite see how you could get another big world into such a small bag, but then, since he hadn't been there himself, he couldn't really tell.

By now the carbon particles were absorbing an enormous amount of heat from the star Hasmon. Slowly at first, then faster and faster, the snow and ice which covered the planet Azuron melted away. Trickles of water began to flow everywhere.

The trickles joined together to form streams, the streams joined together to form rivers, and the rivers joined together to become mighty cascades, which plunged downhill towards the oceans of Azuron.

William, Kiryl and the Professor waited there until all the snow and ice had gone. As if by a stroke of magic, grass sprang forth from the soil that was now revealed.

"You'd have thought everything would have been frozen to death," said William in amazement.

"The seeds of life, when carefully and properly frozen, are immortal," the Professor told him.

Flowers of every description appeared in the grass, and where only a short time before there had been bitter cold, the air was now heavy with many perfumes.

The place where the house from Wit's End had come to rest was near the top of a hill. Below them in the valley other buildings, which had been buried by the snows and ice, could be seen.

"Look!" exclaimed Kiryl, pointing. People were appearing from their homes!

"Were they frozen too?" William asked.

"It seems they were," Gamma replied.

"This must have been what happened on Earth after the ice-ages," William suggested.

"I think this must be where the story of the Sleeping Beauty came from," agreed Kiryl.

Somebody below must have seen the house from Wit's End. A crowd gathered, and William noticed several figures pointing upwards. He was excited at the thought of meeting humanoids from another planet, but the Professor's face was sternly forbidding.

"We must be gone quickly," he said. "This is a simple pastoral society and we are not permitted to disturb it."

47

The return produced no surprises, now that Zero was once again confined to Black-hole Space. They glided easily to Earth along the energy pathways, taking good care to travel backwards in time, so as to arrive at Earth at exactly the moment they had started their outward journey.

They materialised, together with the house in its usual position below the Down at Wit's End. Gamma was much the worse for wear, for his face was badly puffed from the fight with Zero. All three of them were black from head to foot with carbon particles.

"I'll make a cup of tea," Kiryl said cheerfully. Gamma moved to stop her but was too late. The carbon molecules were still banging and popping in the kitchen, and as Kiryl opened the kitchen door William saw a swarm of them surging towards him. Deciding he was already quite dirty enough, he jumped quickly out of the living room through the french windows.

Crossing the snow-covered countryside seemed just as exhausting as it had done before. Ploughing his way through the drifts was slow work, and daylight had almost gone by the time William climbed the fence that surrounded his home garden.

He staggered into the house by the back door, to find his mother there. She was just about to say something when she caught sight of his clothes. "Where on Earth have you been?" she cried in astonishment. She couldn't understand how, on a day of pure white snow, William had contrived to make himself look like a chimney sweep

Without attempting to answer his mother's question, William started to remove his clothes. Then he gathered them into a pile and carried the pile to the outside wash-house.

"Get yourself cleaned up before your father sees you, and don't forget to scrub the bath afterwards," his mother called out after him as William retreated rapidly to the bathroom.

The bath had to be emptied and refilled several times before William became even approximately clean. When at last he was satisfied, he went to a wardrobe to sort out clean clothes. It was only then that he saw himself in a mirror on the wardrobe door. What he saw made him run to his bedroom. It wasn't until he'd jumped into bed and pulled the sheets and blankets up over his head that William paused to think. It must have been the Stopfrost, he decided. And the trouble was, he had no idea how long it would take for the effects to wear off. Instead of their usual deep blue, the stuff had turned his eyes a bright emerald green. *cool.*